Hiya! My name Thudd. Best robot friend of Drewd. Thudd know lots of stuff. How stars get born. Where planets come from. What happened to dinosaurs.

Drewd and Unkie Al like to invent stuff. Unkie invent time machine. Oop! Drewd have snack accident. Drewd and Oody go back to beginning of universe! Want to come? Turn page, please!

Get lost with
Andrew, Judy, and Thudd
in all their exciting adventures!

ANDREW LOST

9

IN TIME

BY J. C. GREENBURG

ILLUSTRATED
BY JAN GERARDI

A STEPPING STONE BOOK™

Random House 🏠 New York

*To Dan, Zack, and the real Andrew,
with a galaxy of love.
To the children who read these books: I wish
you wonderful questions. Questions are
telescopes into the universe!
—J.C.G.*

*To Cathy Goldsmith, with many thanks.
—J.G.*

Text copyright © 2004 by J. C. Greenburg.
Illustrations copyright © 2004 by Jan Gerardi.
All rights reserved under International and Pan-American Copyright
Conventions. Published in the United States by Random House
Children's Books, a division of Random House, Inc., New York, and
simultaneously in Canada by Random House of Canada Limited,
Toronto.

www.randomhouse.com/kids
www.AndrewLost.com

Library of Congress Cataloging-in-Publication Data
Greenburg, J. C. (Judith C.)
In time / by J. C. Greenburg ; illustrated by Jan Gerardi. — 1st ed.
   p.   cm. — (Andrew Lost ; 9)   A Stepping Stone book.
SUMMARY: When Uncle Al is kidnapped by Dr. Kron-Tox and sent to
prehistoric times, Andrew, his cousin Judy, and Thudd the robot try
to use Uncle Al's latest invention, the Time-A-Tron, to rescue him,
and learn firsthand about the origins of the universe.
ISBN 0-375-82949-0 (trade) — ISBN 0-375-92949-5 (lib. bdg.)
[1. Time travel—Fiction. 2. Inventions—Fiction.
3. Universe—Fiction. 4. Cousins—Fiction.] I. Gerardi, Jan, ill.
II. Title. III. Series: Greenburg, J. C. (Judith C.). Andrew Lost ; v 9.
PZ7.G82785 It 2004   [Fic]—dc22   2003025572

Printed in the United States of America
First Edition 10 9 8 7 6 5 4 3 2 1

RANDOM HOUSE and colophon are registered trademarks and A STEPPING
STONE BOOK and colophon are trademarks of Random House, Inc.
ANDREW LOST is a trademark of J. C. Greenburg.

THUDD

CONTENTS

ANDREW'S WORLD

Andrew Dubble

Andrew is ten years old, but he's been inventing things since he was four. Andrew's inventions usually get him into trouble, like the time he shrunk himself, his cousin Judy, and his little silver robot Thudd smaller than a mosquito's toe with the Atom Sucker.

Today a problem with a snack has sent Andrew traveling through time—to the beginning of the universe!

Judy Dubble

Judy is Andrew's thirteen-year-old cousin. At nine o'clock she got into her pajamas in a cabin in Montana. A few minutes later, there wasn't a cabin, there wasn't a Montana . . . there wasn't even an *Earth*!

Thudd

The Handy Ultra-Digital Detective. Thudd is a super-smart robot and Andrew's best friend. Thudd has helped to save Andrew and Judy from deadly octopuses, killer jellyfish, and the giant squid. But can he save them from the explosion of the *sun*?

Uncle Al

Andrew and Judy's uncle is a top-secret scientist. He invented Thudd and the Time-A-Tron time-travel machine. But before he finished the Time-A-Tron, he was kidnapped and hidden in time!

Will Andrew and Judy be able to find him?

The Time-A-Tron

It looks like a giant cooking timer, but it's really a time-travel machine. Too bad Uncle Al got kidnapped before he could make sure it worked!

Doctor Kron-Tox

The mysterious Doctor Kron-Tox invented a time machine, too—the Tick-Tox Box. He's used it to kidnap Uncle Al. But where has Doctor Kron-Tox hidden him? And why?

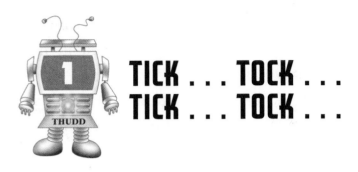

TICK . . . TOCK . . . TICK . . . TOCK . . .

"No onions on my pizza, please," said Andrew Dubble. "They remind me of when we were attacked by snails on the coral reef."

Uncle Al's face crinkled into a smile. "The onions protected you from the snails," said Uncle Al. "They saved your life!"

Andrew and his thirteen-year-old cousin, Judy, were sitting in the big, comfortable kitchen of Uncle Al's log cabin. Just a few hours ago, they had been deep in the Pacific Ocean rescuing a giant squid. Now they were in Montana!

Uncle Al loaded a thick, cheesy slice of

pizza onto a plate. Judy pulled at a string of hot cheese that had gotten tangled in her long, frizzy hair.

"It's too bad we had to leave Hawai'i so fast," she said. "We didn't even have time to eat breakfast."

meep . . . "Uncle Al had to come back," came a squeaky voice from Andrew's shirt pocket. "Big trouble!"

It was Andrew's best friend, Thudd. Thudd was a little silver robot invented by Uncle Al. His name was short for The Handy Ultra-Digital Detective.

Uncle Al nodded. "My partner, Professor Winka Wilde, is missing," he said. "There's a message on the Hologram Helper."

Uncle Al pulled a round purple object the size of a golf ball from his pocket. He pressed a black button at the top of it.

Tick . . . tock . . . tick . . . tock . . .

A whispery voice said:

"Time is short,
Time is long.
Time's a chain.
Its links are strong.

But there's a way
To break time's hold,
To tuck who I want
Into time's many folds.

Miss Wilde is gone.
I'm sure you're vexed.
But don't worry, Dubble!
You'll be next!

Don't look to the future.
Don't study the present.
She's locked in the past,
And it's *sooo* unpleasant!

HA! HA! HA!"

Tick . . . tock . . . tick . . . tock . . .

Judy shivered. "That voice gives me the creeps," she said.

Uncle Al poured grape juice for Judy and Andrew.

"That was a scientist named Doctor Kron-Tox," said Uncle Al. "I used to work with him. He had amazing ideas, but he became obsessed with time. One day, he left our laboratory and vanished without a trace. Now it looks like he kidnapped Winka!"

meep . . . "Unkie Al gotta be careful," said Thudd.

"Don't worry," said Uncle Al. "The worst enemy of a bad problem is a good plan. I'm working on a time machine. It's called the Time-A-Tron, and it's almost ready to test."

"Wowzers schnauzers!" said Andrew. "Where is it?"

meep . . . "Want to see!" said Thudd.

"Well, let's go!" said Uncle Al. He put the Hologram Helper in his pocket and headed for the kitchen door.

Uncle Al's cabin was under a tall pine tree. The land beyond the tree made Andrew think of other planets. The ground was stony and dry. Tall brown rocks stood in rows like weird statues. Scruffy bushes poked up between the rocks.

Uncle Al led the way up a path lit with lights. Andrew and Judy caught up with him at the top of a hill.

Hnnnnnnnnnnnnn . . . came a humming sound from somewhere in the distance.

"It's down there," said Uncle Al.

In the valley below was a giant glowing mushroom!

THUDD

THE TIME-A-TRON

Andrew and Judy followed Uncle Al down the rocky path. As they got closer to the mushroom, they saw it was actually an inflatable dome.

Uncle Al went to a square little box on the wall of the dome and spoke into it. "Good golly, Miss Molly," he said, and part of the wall swung open.

Inside was a small, empty room. Hanging from the ceiling was a giant spiderweb.

"How do you like my burglar alarm system?" asked Uncle Al. "If someone tries to get in without the password, the Catch-O-

Matic web flops down and holds them here."

Uncle Al grinned at Andrew and Judy. "I got the idea when you guys were trapped in the spiderweb in Mrs. Scuttle's bathroom."

Andrew and Judy looked at each other and smiled.

Uncle Al opened a door at the end of the little room.

HNNNNNNNNNNNNN . . .

Now Andrew didn't just *hear* the humming sound. He could *feel* it, too.

The door led into a huge room. In the middle of the room was an enormous egg-shaped object. It almost touched the ceiling!

Andrew's eyes grew wide. "Wowzers schnauzers!" he said. "Is that—"

"The Time-A-Tron!" said Uncle Al proudly.

The top half of the egg was a clear dome. The bottom half was silver. The whole thing sat on a silver cone that floated off the ground.

"Cheese Louise!" said Judy. "It looks like a cooking timer! We have a little one just like it in our kitchen."

"How does the Time-A-Tron work?" Andrew asked Uncle Al.

Uncle Al scratched his chin. "Do you know about the speed of light?"

"Yup," said Judy. "That's how far light can travel in a second."

meep . . . "One hundred and eighty-six thousand miles in one second!" said Thudd.

"That's right!" said Uncle Al. "If you traveled at the speed of light, in just one second you could cross the United States seventy-five times!

"Some people think that light is the fastest thing in our universe. But there is something that can travel faster than light."

"What?" asked Andrew.

meep . . . "Tachyon!" said Thudd.

"Huh?" said Judy.

"TACK-ee-on" flashed across Thudd's screen.

"Right," said Uncle Al. "Tachyons are extremely tiny. They're much smaller than atoms.

"Traveling faster than light does strange things. It may even allow us to travel through time. The Time-A-Tron is fueled by tachyons."

Andrew squinted at the Time-A-Tron. There was a blur in the middle of it.

"Why does the middle of the Time-A-Tron look fuzzy?" he asked.

"That's because of the Fast-Fins," said Uncle Al. "They're moving so quickly you can't see them. The tachyons get the Fast-Fins spinning faster than the speed of light and then . . ."

Andrew started walking toward the back of the Time-A-Tron.

"Andrew!" said Uncle Al. "Don't touch anything!"

"I won't," said Andrew. "But when can we try it?"

"The Fast-Back button is finally working," said Uncle Al. "But the Fast-Forward button is causing trouble. You and Judy can help me with that tomorrow. But only if you promise to follow my instructions exactly."

"We will!" said Andrew.

Judy shook her head. "Andrew, you've messed up every invention you've ever touched," she said. "Look what happened with the Atom Sucker. You got us shrunk smaller than a fly's eye!"

"That wouldn't have happened if you hadn't sneezed," said Andrew.

Judy put her hands on her hips. "And what about when you broke the destination dial off the Water Bug? We ended up sinking to the deepest place in the world!"

"But we saved the giant squid!" said Andrew.

"Come on, guys, don't argue," said Uncle Al. "Why don't you go back to the cabin and get ready for bed? Make yourselves some hot chocolate. I'll be back in ten minutes."

Outside the laboratory, the moon was full and bright. The moonlight made the strange rocks look even stranger.

When they got back to the cabin, they washed up and got into their pajamas. Judy put on her bathrobe, too. Just like his regular clothes, Andrew's pajamas had lots of pockets, and the pockets were full of stuff.

Back in the kitchen, Andrew found the hot chocolate mix. Judy got the milk out of the refrigerator and warmed it up in the microwave. Andrew broke off a big chunk of Uncle Al's gooey chocolate fudge.

They took their snacks into the living room and snuggled into Uncle Al's cozy sofa.

"Better not get any fudge on the sofa," said Judy.

"Don't worry," said Andrew.

He chewed off a big bite, wrapped the rest in a napkin, and tucked it into his pajama pocket next to Thudd.

BOOOOOOH-*HAH!* BOOOOOOH-*HAH!* BOOOOOOH-*HAH!* came an ear-shattering sound from somewhere outside.

"What's that?" asked Judy.

"It's an alarm!" said Andrew.

THUDD

3 THE TICK-TOX BOX

Judy and Andrew ran out of the cabin in their pajamas and slippers. The sound was coming from the laboratory.

BOOOOOOH-*HAH!* BOOOOOOH-*HAH!* BOOOOOOH-*HAH!*

When they got to the laboratory, the door was open. Pieces of the Catch-O-Matic were on the floor of the first room. The only thing caught in it was a piece of paper.

Judy ran into the big room. Andrew found the alarm switch and shut it off.

"ANDREW!" Judy screamed.

"Holy moly!" shouted Andrew when he

saw what was happening in the big room.

Floating in the air next to the Time-A-Tron was a cube-shaped chunk of blackness! Flashes of lightning flickered inside it.

"Uncle Al!" hollered Andrew and Judy.

"Unkie!" squeaked Thudd.

No one answered.

Andrew remembered the paper he'd seen when he came in. He went back to the front room and tugged the paper from the Catch-O-Matic.

The thick, creamy paper was folded and sealed with an old-fashioned wax stamp. Pressed into the wax was the face of a clock.

Andrew tore open the seal and ran back to the big room.

"Look at this!" he said.

Judy read the bold black handwriting:

Time has power,

Time has locks.

Time trapped Dubble

In the Tick-Tox Box.

Silly children,
What can you do?
Your uncle is gone
And you will be, too!

Do you know where he is,
This uncle of yours?
It's a mammoth place
And it's got no doors.

It's terribly cold,
But you need not worry.
There are warm, tusky things
That are horribly furry.

Will his stay be long?
I don't know.
How long can you live
All crusted with snow?

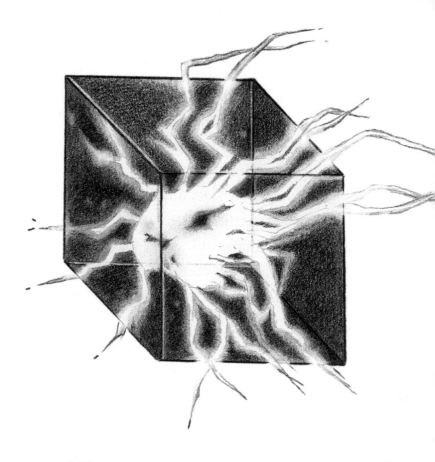

"Oh no!" said Judy. "Doctor Kron-Tox has kidnapped Uncle Al!"

meep . . . "Unkie!" squeaked Thudd.

"That black thing must be the Tick-Tox Box," said Andrew, hurrying back to the big room. "Look what's happening to it!"

The Tick-Tox Box was fading. Now it was only as dark as a storm cloud. The flashes inside of it got dimmer and dimmer until the box disappeared completely.

meep . . . "Understand puzzle!" said Thudd. "Mammoth. Tusky. Uncle Al hidden in time when mammoths live. Could be four million years ago. Or could be four thousand years ago. Mammoths on Earth four million years!"

"Oh great!" said Judy. "I'll just set my alarm clock for four million years ago."

meep . . . "Gotta use Time-A-Tron," said Thudd.

"We don't know *anything* about the Time-A-Tron," said Judy.

"I guess it's time to find out," said Andrew.

4 BLAFOOOOOM!

"Come on, Judy," said Andrew, walking toward the Time-A-Tron.

HNNNNNNNNNNNN . . .

Judy crept toward the Time-A-Tron as though she were sneaking up on a sleeping dragon.

There was a rope ladder hanging down from the Time-A-Tron. It led to an oval door in the bottom. Andrew climbed the ladder. The door didn't have a handle or a lock, but there was a square shape in the middle.

Andrew took a guess.

"Good golly, Miss Molly," he said into the square.

bong . . . The door zipped aside.

HNNNNNNNNNNNNNNNN . . .

The humming sound was even louder.

Andrew crawled inside. Judy crept in after him.

bong . . . The door zipped shut behind them!

"Uh-oh," said Andrew.

It was totally dark.

"Maybe there's a light switch on the wall," said Judy. "I'll feel around."

"Me too," said Andrew, reaching out his hands.

"I found a switch," he said, flipping it.

bong . . . "Tachyons loading," came a deep, echoey voice.

"Oops," said Andrew.

"Turn that switch *OFF,* Bug-Brain!" said Judy.

"I'll try," said Andrew.

"Youch!" yelled Judy, tripping over something on the floor.

"Oofers!" yelled Andrew, tripping into Judy.

Andrew snagged a cord and hung on to it to keep from falling.

bong . . . "Power cord activated," came the deep voice. "Time-A-Tron preparing for time travel. The countdown begins now. One hundred . . . ninety-nine . . . ninety-eight . . ."

"Cheese Louise!" said Judy. "We've got to stop this thing! We don't know what we're doing!"

"Here's another switch," said Andrew, flipping it.

A light went on.

They were in a large, round chamber. In the middle was a spinning black ball. At the bottom of it, black tubes led to a bulgy shape by the wall. A label on the bulgy shape said TACHYONS.

Next to the bulge was a screen with changing colors.

Underneath the screen were rows of switches. Some had big black handles and others had red ones.

The deep voice kept counting down: ". . . fifty-nine . . . fifty-eight . . ."

Andrew noticed a door in the ceiling. He grabbed its handle and pulled. The door opened and a rope ladder fell down. Andrew climbed into the upper compartment of the Time-A-Tron.

He found himself beside a silvery blue chair big enough for two people. In front of the chair was a flat panel. The floor had outlines of black circles and squares.

". . . twenty-three . . . twenty-two . . . twenty-one . . ."

Andrew looked around the compartment. He didn't see any controls.

"I wonder how you operate this thing," he said.

bong . . .

The flat panel opened up. A digital display at the top of the panel blinked "TODAY." Below the display were several buttons blinking red. The two biggest ones were shaped like arrows. The arrow on the left was labeled FAST-BACK. The one on the right said FAST-FORWARD. Between these two buttons was a squiggly one marked WORM-DRIVE.

bong . . . "Three . . . two . . . one," came the deep voice. "Time travel is now possible."

The Fast-Back, Fast-Forward, and Worm-Drive buttons turned green and began to flash.

Andrew scratched his head. "I guess I have to press one of these," he said.

Just then, Judy came up through the door in the floor.

"Don't touch *anything*!" she hollered.

But it was too late. Andrew had already pushed the Fast-Back button.

HNNNN . . . HNNNN . . .

The humming of the Fast-Fins grew louder and louder. Then the sound changed.

WOOHOOOOOO!

It sounded like the howling of a hurricane. Suddenly snowball-sized balls of bright green light started to fly off the Fast-Fins.

BLAFOOOOOM!

HELLO, WE MUST BE GOING!

The Time-A-Tron shook like a monster blender.

Yergghh! thought Andrew. *I feel like a milk shake.*

Andrew took his finger off the Fast-Back button and flopped into the chair. Judy flopped down next to him. It was so soft and squishy, he felt as though he were sinking into a puffy cloud.

The green lights disappeared.

Andrew stared through the clear dome of the Time-A-Tron. They weren't inside Uncle Al's laboratory anymore. It was daytime. They were outdoors!

"Bizarre-o!" said Judy.

The place looked like the valley where Uncle Al's laboratory had been. But there were a lot more trees. The Time-A-Tron was between some pines. Andrew spotted the path that led to Uncle Al's cabin. It was narrower, and there were no lights along the way.

"Look!" said Judy, pointing to a herd of shaggy creatures in the distance. "Buffaloes!"

"Where are we?" asked Andrew.

bong . . . "We are just where we were before, Master Andrew," said the voice. "The Time-A-Tron follows the atoms of Montana through time. The question is *when* are we."

"Then *when* are we?" asked Andrew. "And who are *you*?"

bong . . . "We are in the year 1905," said the voice. "And I am the Time-A-Tron."

"Wowzers!" said Andrew.

"Strange-a-mundo!" said Judy.

meep . . . "Look!" said Thudd, pointing to the top of a hill.

A man in a plaid shirt was riding a beautiful brown horse. At his side was a silvery gray dog.

"That guy looks kind of familiar," said Andrew.

Judy leaned forward to get a better look.

meep . . . "Man is Chief Running Wolf," said Thudd. "Uncle Al's great-grandpa! Drewd and Oody's great-great-grandpa!"

"Oh my gosh!" said Judy. "Uncle Al told us about him. Chief Running Wolf built the cabin. He had a herd of three hundred buffaloes."

meep . . . "And pet wolf," said Thudd.

"Let's get out and say hi," said Andrew.

bong . . . "Must not do that, Master Andrew," said the Time-A-Tron. "We are visitors in time. We must not change anything."

Andrew was puzzled. "We won't change anything," he said. "We'll just talk to Great-Great-Grandpa Running Wolf."

bong . . . "Even talking can change things," said the Time-A-Tron. "Chief Running Wolf would know the future. That might change what he does in his own time.

"Visiting the past is like visiting a store filled with delicate glass. It is safest to look and not touch. If he simply *sees* us, it might change things."

Andrew cocked his head. "We don't want

to mess up the past," he said. "So I guess we'd better leave. But how do we get to the time we need to go to?"

bong . . . "To what time do you wish to go?"

"We've got to find Uncle Al," said Andrew. "Thudd thinks he's trapped in the time of the mammoths."

bong . . . "We arrived here by Tachyon-Drive when you pressed the Fast-Back button, Master Andrew," said the Time-A-Tron. "But to reach the time of the mammoths, we must go back much further. We must travel by wormhole."

"Wormhole!" said Judy. "What's that?"

meep . . . "Wormhole is shortcut through time," said Thudd.

bong . . . "Your silver friend is right," said the Time-A-Tron. "A worm can get to the other side of an apple by crawling around the outside or going straight through the middle. It's a much shorter distance through the middle. We can travel most quickly through time by creating a wormhole."

"Weird-a-roony!" said Judy.

bong . . . "Please buckle up," said the Time-A-Tron. "Wormholes can be frightfully bumpy—and sometimes much worse. Please follow my instructions exactly."

Rooof! Rooof! the wolf barked.

Chief Running Wolf was riding closer to the Time-A-Tron. His eyebrows rose toward his dark hair. He reminded Andrew of Uncle Al.

bong . . . "Oh dear!" sighed the Time-A-Tron. "Chief Running Wolf has seen us. We are now part of his life."

meep . . . "Maybe chief tell kids about strange thing he saw in buffalo field," said Thudd. "Maybe that why chief's kids and grandkids become scientists. To find out what chief saw."

bong . . . "You are wise as well as clever,

little one," said the Time-A-Tron. "Miss Judy, when I count to three, please tap the Fast-Back button once. Master Andrew, you must press the Worm-Drive button and hold it down until 'Four million years ago' flashes on the digital display. Then you must let go of the Worm-Drive immediately."

"Easy," said Andrew.

"Okay," said Judy.

bong . . . "One . . . two . . . three!" Judy tapped the Fast-Back button and Andrew pushed the button for the Worm-Drive.

KRAZAAAAAAAAAAAAAKKK!

Chief Running Wolf and the Montana landscape disappeared as the Time-A-Tron wrapped itself in a cocoon of colored light. Dazzling fireworks—blazing red, sun yellow, burning orange—swirled outside the Time-A-Tron's dome.

Suddenly Andrew began to feel a little . . . ticklish. Something weird was happening. His

hand was still on the Worm-Drive, but it looked far away. His arm was getting thinner!

Uh-oh, thought Andrew. *I think I'm stretching!*

6 SPAGHETTI-FIED!

bong . . . "Zone of spaghetti-fication!" announced the Time-A-Tron. "Extreme gravity! Extreme stretching!"

"Yuck-a-rama!" hollered Judy. "I feel like someone's playing tug-of-war with me!"

Judy looked like stretchy bubble gum.

bong . . . "Beginning Anti-Gravity Control!" said the Time-A-Tron.

In a few seconds, Andrew's hands didn't look so far away anymore. He was shrinking back to normal size.

1 MILLION YEARS AGO . . . read the digital display. 2 MILLION YEARS AGO . . .

3 MILLION YEARS AGO . . .

GALUMP!

The Time-A-Tron jolted as though they had gone over a big bump. Andrew kept the Worm-Drive button pressed, but Thudd went flying out of Andrew's pocket—together with Uncle Al's fudge.

Thudd fell into Andrew's lap. The fudge splattered onto the Time-A-Tron's control panel!

4 MILLION YEARS AGO . . .

Andrew took his finger off the Worm-Drive button. But it didn't pop up. A piece of fudge was jamming it!

5 MILLION YEARS AGO . . .

"Andrew!" yelled Judy. "What's going on?"

"Um, I think the Worm-Drive button is stuck," said Andrew.

Andrew pushed the button again and again.

6 MILLION YEARS AGO . . . 7 MILLION YEARS AGO . . .

Suddenly the numbers began to flash by

so quickly, they were just a blur.

"Oh no!" cried Judy. "You and your stupid fudge!"

Andrew tried to scratch the fudge away from the button with his fingernail. But the more he tried, the more he jammed the fudge between the button and the control panel.

Andrew scooped Thudd up and put him on the control panel.

"Thudd," said Andrew. "You've got pointy little fingers. *You* try unsticking the button."

meep . . . "Okey-dokey, Drewd," said Thudd, scraping.

"Hurry!" cried Judy. "We're going so fast!"

bong . . . *"Emergency!"* The voice of the Time-A-Tron echoed through the compartment. "The Worm-Drive button has been pressed for too long. We are going *TOOOOO FAAAAAR!*"

The Time-A-Tron wobbled in its tunnel of

rainbow fireworks. Thudd jiggled on the control panel, but the suction cups on the bottoms of his feet helped him stick tight.

bong . . . "Terrible trouble!" moaned the Time-A-Tron. "Because of poor judgment about storing chocolate fudge, we are totally out of control."

Suddenly the display blinked a number they could see: 10 BILLION YEARS AGO.

"*YIKES!*" said Andrew. "That's before dinosaurs lived on Earth."

bong . . . "That is five billion years before there *was* an Earth," said the Time-A-Tron.

"You mean there's no *Earth* where we are right now?" asked Judy. "We've got to stop this thing!" She kicked the control panel.

bong . . . "Let us hope our little silver friend is an expert fudge remover," said the Time-A-Tron.

meep . . . "Know how much a billion is?" asked Thudd as he scratched away at the fudge.

"Um, it's a thousand million," said Andrew.

meep . . . "Know what a billion look like?" asked Thudd, scraping and scraping.

"Keep scraping," said Judy.

meep . . . "A billion one-dollar bills make pile ten times high as Mount Everest!" said Thudd. "Fifty-five miles high!"

ll BILLION YEARS AGO flashed on the display.

"What exactly *is* this stupid wormhole anyway?" asked Judy. "And how can we get out of it?"

bong . . . "Do you know what a black

hole is?" asked the Time-A-Tron.

"A hole that's black?" said Judy.

12 BILLION YEARS AGO flashed on the display.

meep . . . "Black hole happen when giant star get old," said Thudd. "Star make big, big explosion. Outside of star blow away. But center of star shrink, shrink, shrink! If Earth shrink as much as star shrink, Earth be size of golf ball!"

"That's ridiculous!" said Judy.

"How can it shrink that much?" asked Andrew.

meep . . . "Gravity," said Thudd. "Gravity pull stuff together. Gravity keep Drewd and Oody stuck to Earth. Gravity keep planets in orbit around sun."

Judy rolled her eyes. "Gravity, shmavity!" she said. "Just make this thing *stop*!"

13 BILLION YEARS AGO flashed on the display.

meep . . . "Black-hole gravity super-super

strong," said Thudd. "Make Drewd and Oody stretch like spaghetti. Black hole pull everything inside. Even light! Can't see black hole. Everything that go inside disappear forever!

"But some black holes like tunnels. Black hole with other end is wormhole. Something go into wormhole at one end. Leave other end in different time, different place."

14 BILLION YEARS AGO blinked on the display.

bong . . . "We go where no one has gone before," said the Time-A-Tron.

"I don't *want* to go where no one has gone before!" said Judy. "Thudd, speed it up with that fudge!"

meep . . . "Trying," said Thudd.

bong . . . "If we arrive at the very beginning of the universe," said the Time-A-Tron, "we won't have to worry about what to do."

"Why?" asked Andrew.

bong . . . "Because we will shatter into trillions of tiny pieces."

THE BIG BANG!

"WHAT?" cried Judy.

"Holy moly!" said Andrew.

bong . . . "But if we arrive a bit after the universe is born, there's a small chance we may survive."

Judy rolled her eyes. "Well, *that* really cheers me up," she said.

bong . . . "If we manage to stop in time, the light will be brighter than billions of suns. You will need special goggles."

A door under the control panel sprang open. Two pairs of goggles fell out. The lenses were thick as bricks.

bong . . . "Hurry, hurry, *HURRY*!" said the

Time-A-Tron. "We are terribly close."

Andrew slid the goggles over his head.

Judy was pulling on her goggles when her eyes suddenly got wide.

"Wait a minute," she said.

She reached for her neck and pulled off a thin silver chain. The chain was looped through a pearly shell that Judy had found on the beach in Hawai'i. The edge of the shell was thin and sharp.

Judy handed the shell to Thudd.

"Try this," she said, slipping the goggles over her eyes.

meep . . . "Okey-dokey," said Thudd.

He poked the edge of the shell around the button.

meep . . . "Got it!" said Thudd, scooping up the last bit of fudge. He held the shell out to Judy.

The Worm-Drive button popped up!

"Super-duper pooper-scooper!" shouted Andrew.

The rainbow colors disappeared. Even through the brick-thick goggles, Andrew could see the light that the Time-A-Tron had warned them about—light brighter than a billion suns!

All at once, it was horribly hot inside the Time-A-Tron. Andrew got so wet with sweat, he felt like a boiled potato.

I'm melting! he thought.

"Where are we?" he asked, woozy with heat.

bong . . . "We are at three minutes after

the universe began," said the Time-A-Tron. "It is incredibly lucky that we stopped here.

"But we have a terrible problem. The Time-A-Tron cannot find any atoms of Montana. That is because atoms do not exist yet. Let us hope the Time-A-Tron can find just a tiny particle of Montana. Then the buttons will blink green and we will be able to leave."

"Humph," said Judy. "I'm hotter than a Thanksgiving turkey, my hair smells like it's burning, and we're stuck at the beginning of the universe. So tell me how we're lucky."

bong . . . "It is only a billion degrees out there now," said the Time-A-Tron.

meep . . . "Ten million times hotter than boiling water!" said Thudd.

bong . . . "Three minutes ago, it was millions of times hotter than that!" said the Time-A-Tron.

"Why is everything so *hot*?" asked Andrew, shaking a shower of sweat out of his hair.

bong . . . "Our universe began in an explosion that is beyond imagination," said the Time-A-Tron.

"I know about that!" said Andrew. "It's called the Big Bang."

bong . . . "Yes, Master Andrew," said the Time-A-Tron. "The Big Bang created enormous heat and energy. But the strangest part is this: The thing that exploded was smaller than an atom. From that tiny thing came everything in the universe—the galaxies, the stars, the planets."

"Cheese Louise," said Judy, fanning her very red face. "That's super-ridiculous! I don't believe it!"

meep . . . "What Time-A-Tron say is true," said Thudd.

bong . . . "Thank you, Thudd," said the Time-A-Tron. "Three minutes after the Big Bang, the only things that exist are parts of atoms and light."

"This light is awful!" said Judy. "Even with these goggles on, it's making my head hurt!"

"You mean there's no stuff to *see* out there?" asked Andrew. "No stars? No planets?"

bong . . . "It will be two hundred million years before there will be things to see in the universe."

Judy folded her arms across her chest and glared at Andrew through her goggles. Drops of sweat were dripping off her nose. "Of all the awful things you've ever gotten us into, Andrew, this is the *awfullest!*"

Andrew shrugged his shoulders. "We have to find Uncle Al and Professor Wilde," he said. "But I guess putting fudge in my pocket wasn't such a good idea."

meep . . . "Fast-Forward button blinking green!" said Thudd.

bong . . . "Ah, but not the Worm-Drive button," said the Time-A-Tron.

Blop!

A fat drop plopped onto the control panel.

Eek! Thudd squeaked, pointing to the Time-A-Tron's window. It was bubbling—and dripping!

Blop!

Another drop of the Time-A-Tron landed on the floor.

bong . . . "We are in a most dangerous situation," said the Time-A-Tron. "Even though this vehicle is made of Strongium, it cannot last long in this heat."

Judy and Andrew leaned over the Worm-Drive button.

Thudd went to the button and gave it a kick.

It started blinking green!

bong . . . "Ahhh!" sighed the Time-A-Tron. "We are forever grateful to you, little friend. And now we are ready to leave the beginning of the universe.

"Miss Judy, at the count of three, please tap the Fast-Forward button. Master Andrew, you will hold down the Worm-Drive button until the display flashes 'Four million years ago.' One . . ."

As Andrew moved his finger toward the blinking button, he could feel terrible heat.

"Two . . ."

"Wait a minute!" said Andrew. "The buttons will be too hot to touch."

Andrew took off his slipper and used it to press the button.

"Good idea!" said Judy.

She took off her slipper and held it over the Fast-Forward button.

bong . . . "We will begin again," said the Time-A-Tron. "One . . . two . . . three!"

"Uh-oh," said Andrew, pressing on his button. "Now the Worm-Drive button won't go *down*!"

8

TWINKLE, TWINKLE, LITTLE STARS

meep . . . "Button too fat," said Thudd. "Heat make stuff get bigger."

A little waterfall of sweat dribbled off Andrew's chin. Andrew pushed the button harder, but it wouldn't budge.

"What do we do now?" he asked, wiping his face with the sleeve of his damp pajamas.

"My father has a way of fixing things," Judy said. She grabbed Andrew's slipper.

Flack!

She tapped the Fast-Forward button and whacked the Worm-Drive button with the heel of her slipper. It went down!

The Fast-Fins spun a web of rainbow-colored light around the Time-A-Tron.

KRAZAAAAAAAAAAAAAKKK!

The Time-A-Tron shook with sound.

"Super-duper pooper-scooper!" yelled Andrew. "We're going!"

Andrew felt that stretchy feeling. He looked over at Judy. She was getting stringy.

We're getting spaghetti-fied again! thought Andrew.

bong . . . "Beginning Gravity Control!" said the Time-A-Tron.

"Whew!" sighed Andrew. "That feels better. And I feel cooler!"

BUH-BUH-BUH-ZNERKKK!

The Time-A-Tron trembled. Then it got very still.

The rainbow lights were gone. Outside the Time-A-Tron, it was perfectly dark.

bong . . . "Ah," sighed the Time-A-Tron. "We have more problems."

"Not again!" said Judy.

bong . . . "We do not have enough fuel to power the Worm-Drive. We will have to travel by Tachyon-Drive alone.

"However, I do have a bit of good news for you. We have traveled three hundred thousand years past the Big Bang. The temperature outside has chilled to three thousand degrees. And you may take off your goggles."

Andrew slipped off his goggles and peered outside into the blackness.

"Is there *anything* out there?" asked Andrew.

bong . . . "Only two kinds of atoms, the smallest ones—hydrogen and helium," said the Time-A-Tron.

"Helium, shmelium!" said Judy. "We've got to get out of here!"

bong . . . "Yes, of course," said the Time-A-Tron. "Miss Judy, you will need to hold down the Fast-Forward button until we arrive at four million years ago."

Judy smacked the Fast-Forward button and held it down.

HNNNN . . . HNNNN . . . WOOHOOOOOOO!

The Time-A-Tron wobbled dizzily and the spinning Fast-Fins threw off balls of bright green light.

BLAFOOOOOM!

bong . . . "Good work, Miss Judy," said the Time-A-Tron. "We are speeding through time again with the atoms of Montana. And since we are not traveling through a wormhole, you will be able to see the universe happen in fast motion. Watch carefully."

Andrew searched the endless blackness hoping to see something—anything. After a while, the display flashed:

12 BILLION YEARS AGO.

"Oh look!" said Judy, pointing through the dome of the Time-A-Tron.

It was an arc of twinkling light.

meep . . . "First stars in our galaxy!" said

Thudd. "Gravity pull gas molecules together. When molecules smoosh together, molecules get hot, hot, hot! Make star!"

bong . . . "Our galaxy, the Milky Way, is being born," said the Time-A-Tron. "It will be an enormous swirl made up of 200 billion stars.

"The galaxy is so enormous, you can see just a bit of it from here," continued the Time-A-Tron. "But there is a way to see more."

A door in the floor opened. Up came a snow globe as large as a pumpkin.

bong . . . "This is the Super-Peeper," said the Time-A-Tron. "It can show what is happening anywhere in the universe."

9 BILLION YEARS AGO flashed on the display.

Inside the Super-Peeper was a brilliant lump of light with glowing arms swirling around it.

Andrew scratched his head. "That shape reminds me of the whirlpool that flushed us down Mrs. Scuttle's toilet."

"Oh ho!" laughed the Time-A-Tron. "You are right, Master Andrew! Most galaxies have a black hole at the center. The parts of the galaxy near the black hole get flushed!"

Suddenly the big purple button in the middle of Thudd's chest started to blink.

"It's Uncle Al!" said Andrew.

Uncle Al used the Hologram Helper to visit Andrew and Judy in emergencies.

Thudd's purple button popped open and a beam of purple light zoomed out.

But there was no hologram at the end of the beam!

HERE COMES THE SUN!

"Where's Uncle Al?" asked Judy. "He's *always* at the end of the beam."

meep . . . "Maybe Hologram Helper not working," said Thudd.

"At least he's alive," said Andrew. "He's got the Hologram Helper and he's trying to send us a message."

"Unless Doctor Kron-Tox has his Hologram Helper," said Judy.

Inside the Super-Peeper, a burst of light lit up one arm of the galaxy.

meep . . . "Exploding star!" said Thudd. "Star is like furnace that heat house. Need fuel. When star use up fuel inside, star die. But not go out like light bulb. Star do strange stuff. Shrink, explode, turn into black hole sometime."

"Are we near that exploding star?" Andrew asked.

Inside the Super-Peeper, a little red arrow lit up far from the exploding star and far from the center of the galaxy. "You are here," glowed a sign above the arrow.

"But there's nothing *there*," said Judy.

bong . . . "That is because our sun and solar system do not exist yet," said the Time-A-Tron. "Now they are simply a floating cloud of gas. We're in the midst of that cloud.

"But in a while a star that is close to us will explode. That explosion will push gas molecules together. Then our sun will begin to be born. When stars explode, they help to make new stars."

meep . . . "Make lotsa other stuff, too!" said Thudd. "Make lotsa kinds of atoms."

bong . . . "Quite right, Master Thudd!" said the Time-A-Tron. "Exploding stars are the factories of the universe. They make big atoms out of little atoms. Without exploding stars, there would not be the atoms to make *you*! So be grateful for exploding stars."

"Whatever," said Judy. "Just as long as they don't do it around me."

The display on the control panel flashed

6 BILLION YEARS AGO.

bong . . . "Hold on tight," said the Time-A-Tron. "At the rate we are going, the solar system will happen soon!"

Suddenly a ball of yellow light exploded across the sky! It was many times bigger than the sun and much brighter. Ribbons of fire curled away from it.

meep . . . "Exploding star close, close, close!" said Thudd.

bong . . . "The end of that star is the beginning of our sun," said the Time-A-Tron. "Watch."

Outside the Time-A-Tron, a cloud of dust was whipping up.

"It's getting stormy out there," said Andrew.

bong . . . "When a star explodes, it creates powerful waves in space," said the Time-A-Tron. "These waves are pushing our cloud of gas and dust into a spinning whirlpool. As we fast-forward through time, you will watch

what happens over thousands of years."

The whirling dust became a huge tornado. Through the storm, a red-orange glow was growing like a huge forest fire.

meep . . . "Sun getting born!" said Thudd. "Lotsa stuff smash together in middle of monster cloud. Get hot, hot, hot!"

bong . . . "Time for your goggles, Dubble children," said the Time-A-Tron. "It will not be long till . . ."

Suddenly the forest-fire sun swallowed up the Time-A-Tron! Rivers of flame were

swirling around it!

"I thought we were following the atoms of Montana!" yelled Judy. "What are we doing *inside the sun?*"

meep . . . "All the stuff that make planets come from sun," said Thudd.

bong . . . "Check your seat belts!" said the Time-A-Tron excitedly. "And you'll need these, too."

A door in the front panel opened and big earplugs dropped out.

"What *now?*" asked Judy.

bong . . . "No time to explain, Miss Judy," said the Time-A-Tron. "Please do as I say."

"Oh, all right," said Judy. "Thudd, get over here and hold down the Fast-Forward button."

Thudd marched up to the button and sat on it.

Judy slapped in her earplugs and folded her arms across her chest. "Humph," she grumped. "It's always something."

BUH-BUH-BUH-BOOOOOOOOM!

Suddenly Andrew felt so heavy, he couldn't move. He could barely breathe. The Time-A-Tron was zooming backward at an incredible speed.

Andrew was too squashed to speak.

bong . . . "It's the sun," groaned the Time-A-Tron. "It's exploding!"

THIS PLANET ROCKS!

"WHAT?" said Judy, pulling out her earplugs.

meep . . . "Sun exploding," said Thudd. "That what baby star do before it turn into grown-up star. Exploding sun throw lotsa stuff far, far away! Stuff go into orbit around sun. Make planets!"

bong . . . "That is right," said the Time-A-Tron. "We have followed our Montana atoms ninety-three million miles from the sun. This is where the Earth will be."

Outside the window was a swirling storm of pebbles. Then came rocks. A boulder the size of a bus was headed for them!

"Uh-oh!" said Andrew, ducking down in his seat.

bong . . . "You need not be frightened," said the Time-A-Tron. "As long as we are traveling through time, nothing outside can harm us. Danger happens when we stop."

The bus-sized boulder smashed into a truck-sized boulder. Instead of cracking apart, the rocks stuck together.

"Yowzers!" yelled Andrew.

meep . . . "Rocks hit hard!" said Thudd. "Press together hard, hard, hard! Pressure make heat. Rock melt. Rocks stick together!"

Now some of the rocks zooming around the Time-A-Tron were the size of houses. Then they were the size of schools!

meep . . . "Chunks keep smashing together. Thousands of years!" said Thudd. "Get big, big, big! Make tiny planet. Tiny planets smash together, make big planet!"

bong . . . "We are so very lucky to be where

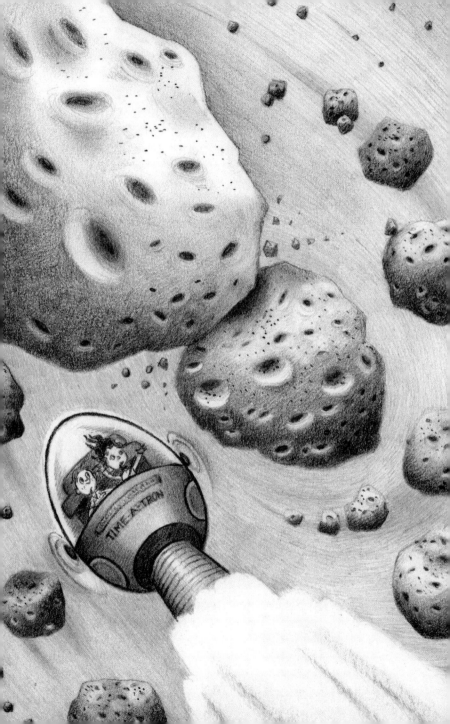

we are," sighed the Time-A-Tron.

"Lucky!" said Judy. "You think we're *lucky* to be in the middle of crashing rocks the size of Texas?"

bong . . . "We are lucky that the Earth will be ninety-three million miles away from the sun," said the Time-A-Tron. "If Earth were closer to the sun or farther away, life would not happen.

"Mercury is thirty-six million miles away from the sun. But it will be so hot that everything will boil away except metal and rock. There will be no water on Mercury. There will be no air to breathe. During the day, the temperature will be eight hundred degrees Fahrenheit."

Suddenly Thudd's purple button popped open. A purple beam zoomed out, but no one was at the end of it.

Tick . . . tock . . . tick . . . tock . . .

A whispery voice began to speak:

"You think you're getting closer.
I assure you that you're not.
Your uncle's getting awfully cold.
Miss Wilde's in a gruesome spot.

But what can Dubble children do
When time is running out?
While stuck inside the Time-A-Tron,
They sit around and pout!

HA! HA! HA!"

Tick . . . tock . . . tick . . . tock . . .

The purple beam vanished. Andrew and Judy looked at each other.

Judy shivered. "It's scary that Doctor Kron-Tox is talking to us with the Hologram Helper," she said.

meep . . . "Unkie gonna be okay," said Thudd quietly.

BUH . . . BUH . . . BUH . . . ZNERKKK! came a sound from deep inside the Time-A-Tron.

The Fast-Fins stopped spinning and the Time-A-Tron stopped lurching.

bong . . . "Oh dear," said the Time-A-Tron. "We are no longer speeding through time. We are stuck in it."

"I'll fix that," said Judy. "Thudd, hop off the button."

She gave the Fast-Forward button a hard smack with her slipper. The Fast-Fins fluttered a little, shook off a few sparks, then stopped.

BUH-BUH-BUH-ZNERKKK!

bong . . . "Good try, Miss Judy," said the Time-A-Tron. "But that got us only ten thousand years ahead. We're stuck in time again."

Andrew scratched his head. "Uncle Al was having trouble with the Fast-Forward button," he said. "He was going to fix it tomorrow."

meep . . . "Look out!" squeaked Thudd, pointing to a mountain speeding toward the Time-A-Tron.

It zoomed closer. It was just a whisker

away. It snagged one of the Fast-Fins!

Judy whacked the Fast-Forward button again and again, but nothing happened.

The Fast-Fins weren't moving at all.

4 BILLION 500 MILLION YEARS AGO flashed the display.

Speeding from behind was another humongous chunk bigger than the mountain they were stuck to!

"We've got to get out of the way!" said Judy, giving the Fast-Forward button another whack.

bong . . . "I do apologize," said the Time-A-Tron. "This is a Time-A-Tron, not a Space-A-Tron."

KRAAAAAAAAXXX!

The humongous chunk smashed into the Time-A-Tron and the mountain it was stuck to. Lightning flashed as the rocks ground against each other—and melted. The Time-A-Tron was getting buried in stone!

Orange lights blinked on and off inside the Time-A-Tron.

"Oh no!" said Judy. "We're trapped!"

meep . . . "Hope Time-A-Tron shell not crack!" said Thudd.

bong . . . "Checking, checking," said the Time-A-Tron.

Holy moly! thought Andrew. *What happens if we get stuck inside the Earth in a broken Time-A-Tron?*

TO BE CONTINUED IN ANDREW, JUDY, AND THUDD'S
NEXT EXCITING ADVENTURE:

ANDREW LOST
ON EARTH!

In stores February 2005

TRUE STUFF

THUDD

Thudd wanted to tell you more about the universe, but he was too busy scraping at fudge. Here's what he wanted to say:

• It's hard to imagine big numbers like millions and billions. Here are some ways to help you think about them: If you counted one dollar bill every second, it would take more than eleven days to count one million dollars—and that's if you didn't sleep!

In thirty-one years, you will be one billion seconds older than you are now.

If there are sixty seconds in a minute, how many seconds are in an hour? A day? A year?

• Huge distances in the universe are often measured in light-years. A light-year is the number of miles light can travel in one year, almost 6 *trillion* miles. A trillion is 1,000 billion!

• The speed of sound changes with temperature. At room temperature, sound can travel 1,130 feet in one second. Light can travel 186,000 *miles* in one second. That's 870,000 times faster!

• Scientists have figured out that the universe exploded into existence more than 14 billion years ago. But no one knows what existed before then!

• As the Time-A-Tron says, we are lucky to be 93 million miles from the sun. Living things—at least the ones we know about—can exist only if there is water. Mercury and Venus are so hot during the day that all the water has boiled away.

• Mars is about 50 million miles farther away from the sun than we are. It is much colder than Earth, and its water is frozen. But when Mars was a young planet, it was warmer and water flowed! Some scientists think that life may once have existed on Mars. They're still looking!

• Mars looks red when you see it through a telescope. That's because there's lots of iron in Mars's soil—and it's rusty!

• When the baby sun exploded, the heavy stuff stayed close to the sun. That's what makes up Mercury, Venus, Mars, and Earth. A lot of the lighter stuff—gases like helium—drifted much farther away from the sun. That's why Jupiter, Saturn, and Uranus are giant balls of gas!

• Jupiter is enormous. You could fit more than a thousand Earths inside it!

• Black holes have so much gravity that some of them suck up stars like vacuum cleaners!

Find out more about the planets and see some great pictures—go to www.nasa.gov!

WHERE TO FIND MORE TRUE STUFF

Want to find out more unbelievably strange things about the universe? Read these books!

• *Universe* by Robin Kerrod (New York: DK Publishing, 2003). You'll see what's happening in our solar system and in galaxies trillions of miles away!

• *Time and Space* by John R. Gribbin and Mary Gribbin (New York: DK Publishing, 2000). If you're interested in wormholes, time travel, and how space and time are related, you'll really enjoy this book!

• *The Reader's Digest Children's Atlas of the Universe* by Robert Burnham (Pleasantville,

NY: Reader's Digest Children's Publishing, Inc., 2000). You'll find great pictures, amazing facts, activities, and suggestions for viewing the skies yourself!

Turn the page
for a sneak peek at
Andrew, Judy, and Thudd's
next exciting adventure—

ANDREW LOST
ON EARTH!

Available February 2005

BURIED ALIVE!

KEEERAAACKKK! GRAAACKKK!

"Holy moly!" hollered Andrew Dubble. "It feels like an earthquake out there!"

Giant space rocks were crashing into the Time-A-Tron. It was getting buried deeper and deeper in solid stone!

meep . . . "Baby Earth getting born," squeaked a voice from the control panel of the Time-A-Tron.

It was Thudd, Andrew's little silver robot and best friend.

meep . . . "When baby sun explode, make lotsa space junk—asteroids and comets. Space junk crash! Crash hard! Stick together. Make baby Earth. Make other planets, too!"

Judy, Andrew's thirteen-year-old cousin, rolled her eyes.

"Well, I wish the Earth would get born somewhere else," said Judy.

She was sitting next to Andrew on a big cushy chair in front of the Time-A-Tron's control panel.

KRUNK! Another asteroid clunked outside.

The Time-A-Tron jerked with the crash.

"This is all your fault, Bug-Brain," said Judy. "If your stupid fudge hadn't gotten stuck on the Fast-Back button, we wouldn't have gone back to the beginning of the universe in our pajamas!"

meep . . . "Just got five billion years to go!" said Thudd. "Then we be back home!"

bong . . . "If we have enough tachyon fuel to get there," said the Time-A-Tron in a deep, echoey voice.

"Cheese Louise!" said Judy. "We're getting buried deeper inside the Earth every minute! We've got to get out of here!"

bong . . . "I do apologize, Miss Judy," said the Time-A-Tron. "But all we can do is follow the molecules of Montana."

"Super-duper pooper-scooper!" said Andrew. "That means we'll end up back in Montana!"

bong . . . "Unless we end up buried many miles deep *under* Montana," said the Time-A-Tron.

"Uh-oh," said Andrew. "I didn't think of that."

"Bummer!" said Judy.

meep . . . "Drewd! Oody! Look!" said Thudd, pointing to the Super-Peeper. "Something big coming!"

The Super-Peeper showed something monstrously huge streaking toward the Time-A-Tron.

"It's going so fast!" said Judy. "We're toast!"

bong . . . "You will need these," said the Time-A-Tron.

Two pairs of earplugs dangled from a door in the control panel. But before Andrew and Judy could put them on . . .

KEEERUUUCK! came a sound so loud it hurt Andrew's ears.

The Time-A-Tron shook like a train wreck. *SPLURSH!*

The rocks around the Time-A-Tron glowed red and swirled by the window.

meep . . . "Giant rock hit hard. Make lotsa heat! Melt lotsa rock!" said Thudd. "Stuff that hit make heat. Clapping hands make little heat. Big stuff make lotsa heat."

"Clap a lid on it, Thudd!" said Judy. "What if all this hot rock melts the Time-A-Tron like when we were near the beginning of the universe?"

bong . . . "It was a billion degrees near the beginning of universe, Miss Judy," said the Time-A-Tron. "This rock soup is only two thousand degrees."

Judy slammed the heel of her slipper on the Fast-Forward button.

Flack! Flack! Flack!

HNNNNN . . . HNNNN . . . WOO-HOOOOOOO!

The Time-A-Tron jiggled in the molten mud. Andrew could feel a vibration as the Fast-Fins began to spin. Sparks of bright green light flashed outside the Time-A-Tron.

"Green sparks!" said Andrew. "The Fast-Fins are working!"

BLAFOOOOOOM!

bong . . . "We're off!" said the Time-A-Tron.

BUH-BUH-BUH-ZNERKKK!

They could feel the Fast-Fins slowing down. The green sparks disappeared.

bong . . . "Oh dear!" said the Time-A-Tron. "We've moved only ten thousand years ahead. That whack should have gotten us at least ten *million* years further!"

The hot rock still gushed and swirled around the Time-A-Tron and was slowly pushing it.

"Look!" said Andrew, pointing to the top of the Time-A-Tron's dome. "I think I see stars!"

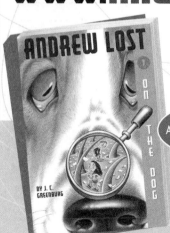